This Annual belongs to

Rebekah Newman

How many of our shadows can you find behind the page numbers? The answer is at the end of the story!

Editor: Anne Ewart   Designer: Martin Shubrook and Paul Shubrook

Published in Great Britain in 2003 by Egmont Books Limited, 239 Kensington
High Street, London, W8 6SA. Printed in the U.A.E. ISBN 07498 5907 5

THE LION KING

CONTENTS

DISNEY THE LION KING

The sun came up over the African plain just as it had done since the beginning of time. But today something was different.

The first rays of the morning sun shone down on an amazing sight. Hundreds of animals were moving in a grand parade across the Pride Lands.

Elephants plodded, antelope ran, giraffes loped and cheetahs raced. Ants marched in an orderly line while flocks of flamingos flew gracefully across the sky.

They were all travelling to Pride Rock to celebrate the birth of the Lion King's son.

Above the gathering, on top of Pride Rock, Rafiki, the ancient baboon, approached King Mufasa and Queen Sarabi. He cracked open a special fruit and made a mark on the tiny cub's forehead with its juice.

Then he carried the cub to the edge of the rock and held him high, "We welcome Simba, our future king, to the Circle of Life!" proclaimed Rafiki.

Cheers rose across the plain as the animals joined in the welcome.

That afternoon, Zazu, the King's adviser, flew to see Mufasa's brother, Scar. "You'd better have a good excuse for missing this morning's ceremony," said Zazu. "You should have been first in line!"

"I was first in line – for the throne!" snarled Scar. "Then that hairball Simba came along and spoilt my chances!" he added, in disgust.

The days passed and Simba grew from an infant into a lively cub.

Early one morning, as the sun was rising, Mufasa took Simba to the top of Pride Rock. "Simba, look," said Mufasa, proudly. "Everything the light touches is our kingdom. Some day it will all be yours."

"It's enormous, Father!" gasped Simba, excitedly. "Do you think I'll be able to rule it all?"

"Yes," said Mufasa, "as long as you remember that everything you see exists together in a delicate balance – a great Circle of Life. As the King, you will have to take your place in the Circle and help to preserve that delicate balance."

"Father," asked Simba, looking out towards the horizon, "what's that shadowy place out there?"

Mufasa turned to his son. "That shadowy place is beyond our borders," said Mufasa. "You must never go there."

"Uncle Scar, guess what?" said Simba. "I'm going to be King one day and Father's just shown me our whole kingdom!"

"Really?" said Scar, and a nasty plan began to form in his mind. "Did he show you what lay past the northern border?"

"No," Simba admitted. "He said I must never go there."

"And he's absolutely right!" Scar declared. "Only the bravest lions go there. An elephant graveyard is no place for a young prince!"

Wow! thought Simba. *An elephant graveyard!*

"Promise me you'll never visit that dreadful place," said Scar and, grinning slyly, he sloped off.

Simba stared at the distant spot on the horizon. He didn't realise that Scar had cleverly set a trap to rid himself of the future King, forever!

Just then, Zazu arrived. "Sire!" he cried. "Hyenas have crossed into the Pride Lands!"

The King ordered Zazu to take Simba home. "Please let me come with you, Father," begged Simba.

"No," said Mufasa. "It's too dangerous!" And he rushed away.

A short time later, Simba was scrambling up Pride Rock when he met Scar, sunning himself on a ledge.

Simba knew that he shouldn't disobey his father. But Uncle Scar had said that only the *bravest* lions went to the elephant graveyard. And wouldn't the King be proud of such a brave cub?

Simba dashed off in search of his best friend, a female lion cub named Nala.

He found her with her mother and Queen Sarabi. "Mother," said Simba to Sarabi, "I just heard about this really terrific place. Can Nala and I go, please?"

"Where is this really terrific place, Simba?" asked his mother.

"Er, near the waterhole," Simba lied. He knew Uncle Scar would be angry if he told her the truth.

"All right," said Sarabi, "as long as Zazu goes with you."

Oh, no! thought Simba. *Zazu will spoil everything!*

"We've got to get rid of Zazu!" Simba whispered to Nala.

"Just look at the two of you, sharing secrets!" said Zazu. "Your parents will be thrilled. You're going to be married one day!"

"I can't marry Nala!" cried Simba. "She's my friend! When I'm the King, I'll do just as I please!"

"With that attitude you won't be a very good king!" said Zazu, sternly.

"I can't wait to be King," laughed Simba and he darted into a herd of zebras. Nala followed and the pair successfully escaped from Zazu!

"It worked! We lost him!" boasted Simba. "Now we can look for the elephant graveyard!"

"I think we've found it," said Nala. "Look!"

In the mist ahead they could see a huge elephant skull. "It's really creepy," said Nala.

"Come on," said Simba. "Let's check it out."

But Zazu caught up with them. "Leave here, immediately!" he squawked. "This is beyond the boundary of the Pride Lands and we're all in great danger!"

"I laugh in the face of danger!" boasted Simba. "Ha, ha!"

"Hee, hee!" came the reply, from inside the elephant skull! And suddenly, out of the two eyeholes sprang three, drooling hyenas.

"Well, well," said one hyena, called Shenzi. "What have we got here, Banzai?"

"I don't know, Shenzi," answered Banzai. "What do you think, Ed?"

Ed, the third hyena, just licked his lips.

Baring their fangs, the hyenas crept towards the intruders. But when Shenzi threatened Nala, Simba smacked the hyena across her nose.

"Ow!" screeched Shenzi. "I'll get you for that!"

"Nala, run!" yelled Simba, as the hyenas bounded after them.

The two cubs found themselves trapped inside a gigantic rib cage. Fangs gleaming, the angry hyenas advanced towards Simba.

Suddenly, a giant paw struck Shenzi on the head, sending her and the other hyenas hurtling into a pile of elephant bones.

"Don't you ever come near my son again!" roared Mufasa, as the hyenas ran away as quickly as they could.

Later, when they were alone, Mufasa turned to Simba. "I'm very disappointed in you," he said.

Simba looked very ashamed. "I was just trying to be brave like you, Father," he said.

"I'm only brave when I have to be, said Mufasa. "Being brave doesn't mean you go looking for trouble."

Overhead, stars began to twinkle. "Father, we'll always be together, won't we?" asked Simba, as he walked beside Mufasa.

"Simba, let me tell you something my father told me," said Mufasa, gently. "Look up at the sky. The great Kings of the past look down at us from those stars. They will always be there to guide you. And so will I."

Continued on page 20...

Hyena chase

Can you lead Simba and Nala through the maze to safety? Be careful you don't run into the nasty hyenas along the way!

Splash!

Can you help Nala follow the code to add a splash of colour to this picture of Simba chasing Zazu?

Playtime!

Simba and Nala have the whole of the Pride Lands to run around in.
Play this game with your friends and follow their trail of adventure.
But watch out for Zazu – you don't want him putting a stop to your fun!

1 START 2 3

Take an ostrich ride the wrong way! Go back 4.

25 26 27 23

29 30 31 32

Count the zebras as they run past! Throw again.

34

How to play

Place a counter each on START. Take it in turns to roll a dice and move your counter along the trail obeying any instructions you land on. If you land on Zazu, miss a turn. The first player to reach FINISH is the winner!

Jump along the crocodiles' jaws! Forward 6.

Stop to splash around with the flamingos! Miss 2 turns.

Get caught by Mufasa in the Elephant Graveyard! Go back to Start.

FINISH

Pride Land poses

Simba has so much energy that he's always on the move. Look at the words at the bottom of the page and pick the one that best describes each picture.

sleeping climbing

pouncing walking

hiding sitting

Scar's shadows

Which slinky shadow matches Scar exactly?

1

2

3

4

5

6

7

Answer: Shadow 5.

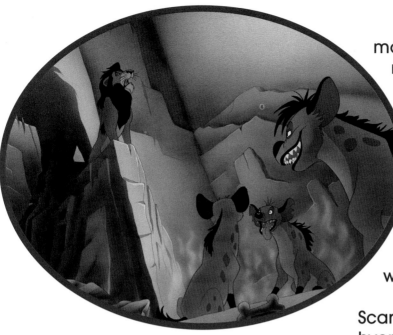

"No, I'm not kidding, you mongrels," replied Scar. "Listen to me! I have another plan…"

The next morning, Scar put his plan into action. He found Simba and led him down into a deep gorge.

"What are we doing here, Uncle Scar?" asked Simba.

"Your father has a marvellous surprise for you," Scar explained. "Just wait here while I fetch him."

But instead of fetching Mufasa, Scar dashed off to find the three hyenas. He needed to let them know that it was time to put his new plan into action.

A herd of wildebeest was grazing peacefully in the gorge. When the hyenas saw Scar's signal, they did as Scar had instructed and charged straight into the herd.

That night, Scar went to see the hyenas. "You idiots!" he shouted. "I gave you the perfect opportunity to get rid of that pest, Simba. And you could have killed Mufasa, too!"

"Kill Mufasa?" exclaimed Shenzi. "Are you kidding?"

The wildebeest were startled by the hyenas and began to stampede through the gorge.

Simba was right in the path of the huge beasts!

Quickly, Simba clawed his way on to a branch. But as the herd thundered past, the branch cracked!

Nearby, Mufasa and Zazu noticed a thick cloud of dust rising from the gorge.

"Mufasa!" yelled Scar, suddenly appearing from behind a rock. "Quick! There's a stampede and Simba's trapped down there!"

"I'm coming, Son!" shouted Mufasa, leaping into the gorge. He grabbed the terrified cub in his mouth and carried him to safety.

But, just as Simba was safe, Mufasa was knocked down by a galloping wildebeest.

Injured and in pain, Mufasa struggled to pull himself out of the deep gorge. "Scar, help me," he panted, as he tried to claw his way to the top.

Scar leaned over the edge and looked down. "Long live the King!" he snarled, viciously.

Then, with a deadly shove, Scar flung Mufasa back to the bottom of the gorge, into the path of the stampeding wildebeest!

As soon as the wildebeest had gone, Simba raced down to his father. "Father! Father!" cried Simba. But there was no reply.

Sobbing, Simba nuzzled Mufasa's still body. The great Lion King was dead.

Scar appeared beside Simba. "What have you done?" he said, menacingly.

"It was an accident!" wailed Simba, loudly.

"If the King hadn't tried to save you, he'd still be alive," Scar snarled. "You must run away and never return!"

Heartbroken and confused, Simba fled.

Immediately, Scar sent the hyenas after Simba with orders to kill him. But Simba managed to outrun them. "We'll get you if you ever come back!" they called after him.

Certain that Simba had been killed, Scar returned with the news to Pride Rock. Sarabi and the other lionesses wept when they heard that the King and the Prince were dead.

Slowly, Scar climbed up to Mufasa's throne. "It is with a heavy heart that I become your new King," announced Scar, solemnly.

Rafiki, shaking his head in disbelief, walked away.

Simba, injured and exhausted, stumbled across the blazing, hot African wasteland. At last, unable to go any further, he fell to his knees and fainted.

Hungry vultures circled above him, waiting to swoop down for their afternoon meal.

But when Simba opened his eyes, the burning sun and the vultures had gone and a meerkat and a warthog were standing over him!

"You nearly died," said the warthog. "We saved you!"

"Thanks for your help," said Simba, standing up shakily, before turning to leave.

"Where are you from, kid?" asked the meerkat.

"It doesn't matter," replied Simba, miserably. "I can't go back there."

"Then stay here with us!" cried the meerkat. "My name's Timon, and this is Pumbaa. Take my advice, kid. Put your past behind you. Hakuna matata – no worries! That's what we say!"

Simba liked his two new, funny friends so he decided to stay with them in the jungle.

As Timon offered Simba some of his big, juicy bugs to eat, the meerkat said, "You'll see, you'll love it here. Just remember – hakuna matata!"

Continued on page 30...

Extreme close-up

Can you tell who is in each of these close-ups?

Answer: 1 - Zazu, 2 - Timon, 3 - Simba, 4 - Rafiki, 5 - Pumbaa, 6 - Scar.

Bug-tastic!

Join the dots to finish this humungous bug
before adding some mouthwatering colours.

Hakuna matata

It's party time in the jungle, so jump up and join in with Timon and Pumbaa's fun!

Fun search

Can you find each of these party words in the word search?

PARTY   **JUNGLE**

FUN   **DANCE**

MUSIC   **GAMES**

```
P A R T Y S
C O J M T P P
Z G U Q A M
D A N C E U
J M G S F S
U E L N U I
N S E R N C
```

All you need to have fun is a big smile!

Jungle juice

After all that dancing, here's how you can make a cool, jungle juice!

You will need: a tall glass, orange juice, Grenadine, sweet bugs, glacé cherries, a cocktail stick and decorations.

1

Push some cherries and sweet bugs on to a cocktail stick.

2

Pour some fresh, cold, orange juice into a tall glass.

3

Pour a small amount of Grenadine into the orange juice.

4

Balance your cocktail stick on top and add the decorations.

5 Your jungle juice is now ready to slurp!

Gee! It's tiring stuff this relaxing business!

27

Greedy guzzlers

Who will be smacking their lips around the most tasty bugs – Timon or Pumbaa? Count the number of bugs on each line to find out!

Timon

Pumbaa

28

Answer: Pumbaa.

Spot the differences

Timon likes spot the differences as much as he likes taking it easy under the stars. Can you spot all ten differences in the bottom picture?

Answer:

1) Missing star. 2) Extra star. 3) Simba's tail moved. 4) Pumbaa's ear. 5) Colour of the moon. 6) Timon is holding a bug. 7) Extra tree. 8) Missing footprint. 9) Edge of rock face. 10) Pumbaa's arm.

29

...Continued from page 23

The years passed very happily for Simba and he grew into a strong and handsome young lion.

One morning, Simba heard his friends shouting for help. He hurried to their cries and found Pumbaa stuck underneath a fallen tree and Timon trying to protect him from a hungry young lioness.

Simba rushed forward and wrestled the lioness away from them.

"Simba?" asked the lioness.
"Nala?" replied Simba.
The lions hugged, overjoyed to have found each other again.
"What's going on?" asked Timon.
Simba laughed and introduced Nala to his friends.
"Everyone thinks you're dead, Simba. Scar told us about the stampede," said Nala.
"What else did he tell you?" asked Simba, cautiously.
"What else matters? You're alive! And that means you're the King!" exclaimed Nala.
"King?" cried Timon and Pumbaa in surprise.
Later, Simba and Nala walked through the jungle. "Scar let the hyenas take over the Pride Lands," said Nala. "Things are terrible. There's no food, no water. Simba, you've got to come back and help."

"I can't go back," insisted Simba.

"Why not?" asked Nala. "Simba, what's happened to you? Why are you hiding from your responsibilities? What would your father think?"

"My father is dead," said Simba, and he turned and walked away.

That night, Simba gazed up at the star-filled sky. *I can never go back*, he thought. "And even if I did go back," he said aloud, "it wouldn't do any good. I'm not you, Father. I never will be."

Suddenly, as if from nowhere, Rafiki appeared.

"Who are you?" asked Simba.

"The question is, who are you?"

replied Rafiki. "I know your father. Come. I will take you to him."

Amazed, Simba followed Rafiki to a still, clear pool. "Look down there," said Rafiki.

But all Simba could see was his own reflection.

"Look harder," encouraged Rafiki.

Suddenly, Simba saw his father's face.

"You see? He lives in you!" said Rafiki.

Then, Simba heard a voice call his name. He looked up and there, in the stars, was the image of his father.

"Look inside yourself, Simba," said the image. "You must take your place in the Circle of Life. Remember who you are. You are my son, and the one true King. Remember..."

"Me, too!" said Pumbaa

Timon hesitated but finally he, too, decided to follow Simba to Pride Rock.

Ahead of them all, Simba was crossing into his homeland – the Pride Lands. Everywhere he looked he saw devastation and ruin.

For a moment, Simba paused, wondering if he should turn back and continue his life with Timon and Pumbaa while he still could. But then, Simba felt a fresh wind and his hope was restored. He continued on towards Pride Rock.

Soon, Nala, Pumbaa and Timon also reached the Pride Lands. They were met by some ferocious hyenas but Timon and Pumbaa managed to distract them while Nala went on to find the lionesses.

The next morning, Rafiki came to see Nala, Timon and Pumbaa. "The King has returned," he told them.

"What do you mean?" asked Timon, worried.

"Simba has gone back to Pride Rock to challenge his uncle," exclaimed Nala, happily. "I'm going with him!"

Meanwhile, at Pride Rock, Scar was continuing his reign of terror. "Where is your hunting party?" he bellowed at Sarabi.

"There is nothing to hunt," she replied. "The herds have moved on. Our only hope is to leave Pride Rock."

"We're not going anywhere," growled Scar.

"Then you are sentencing us to death," said Sarabi.

"So be it!" said Scar. "I am the King and I make the rules!"

"If you were half as good a King as Mufasa was…" began Sarabi.

Enraged, Scar struck her and she fell to the ground.

All at once, a mighty roar echoed through the rocks. Scar whirled round and saw a great lion standing before him.

"Mufasa?" gasped Scar. "No! It can't be! You're dead!" Scar back away, terrified. He thought he was seeing a ghost. "Why are you here?" he whimpered. "Go away! Leave me alone!"

Even though many years had passed, Sarabi still recognised her son. "Simba, you're alive!" she said quietly.

"Yes, and I have come to reclaim my kingdom," declared Simba. "Step down, Scar."

Simba, who was struggling to keep his hold on the rock. "Now, where have I seen this before?" Scar sneered. "Oh, yes. I remember. This is the way your father looked, just before I killed him."

At last, Simba knew the truth!

With renewed strength, Simba drew himself up and leapt at Scar.

Scar called for the hyenas to come to his help. But Nala and the lionesses had arrived with Timon and Pumbaa. With fury, they attacked the hyenas and drove them away.

As the groups clashed, lightning struck the dry grass of the Pride Lands plain. The wind swept huge flames towards Pride Rock.

With the hyenas gone, Simba saw Scar crawling up to the top of Pride Rock.

Dodging the blaze, Simba dashed up the steep face and trapped Scar at the edge.

Scar laughed. "Well, I would, of course, but there is one little problem," he said, gesturing towards the hyenas.

Suddenly, the hyenas leapt at Simba. He tried to fight them off but there were too many. The hyenas forced Simba to the edge of the cliff.

"Enough!" cried Scar. He padded over and looked down at

"Please don't hurt me," begged Scar. "The hyenas killed your father. They're the enemy, Simba. I'm your family!"

Simba paused for a moment. "Run away, Scar. Run away and never return!" he whispered.

Scar started to slink away. Then suddenly, he turned and lunged at Simba.

Acting quickly, Simba hurled Scar off the cliff. The angry hyenas, waiting at the bottom of the cliff, killed their defeated master.

As rain began to fall, Simba climbed to the top of Pride Rock. The clouds parted, revealing a sky gleaming with stars.

Simba roared triumphantly and all the animals who heard him felt a surge of hope rise within them.

Soon, under the rule of King Simba, the herds returned to the Pride Lands and there was plenty of food and water for all.

Then, one day the animals gathered from across the Pride Lands to celebrate the birth of King Simba and Queen Nala's new son.

As Rafiki held the cub high over Pride Rock, Simba thought of his father and remembered his love and wisdom. Then, with happiness in his heart, he welcomed his son to the unbroken Circle of Life.

The end!

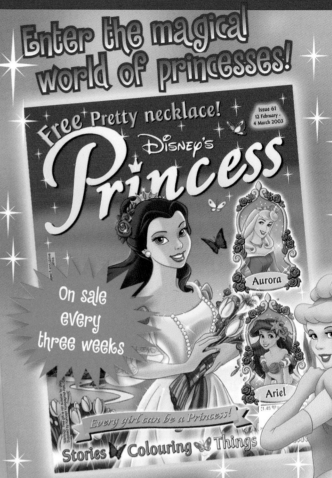

This Annual belongs to

Rebekah Newman

How many of our shadows can you find behind the page numbers? The answer is at the end of the story!

4

Disney's THE JUNGLE BOOK 2

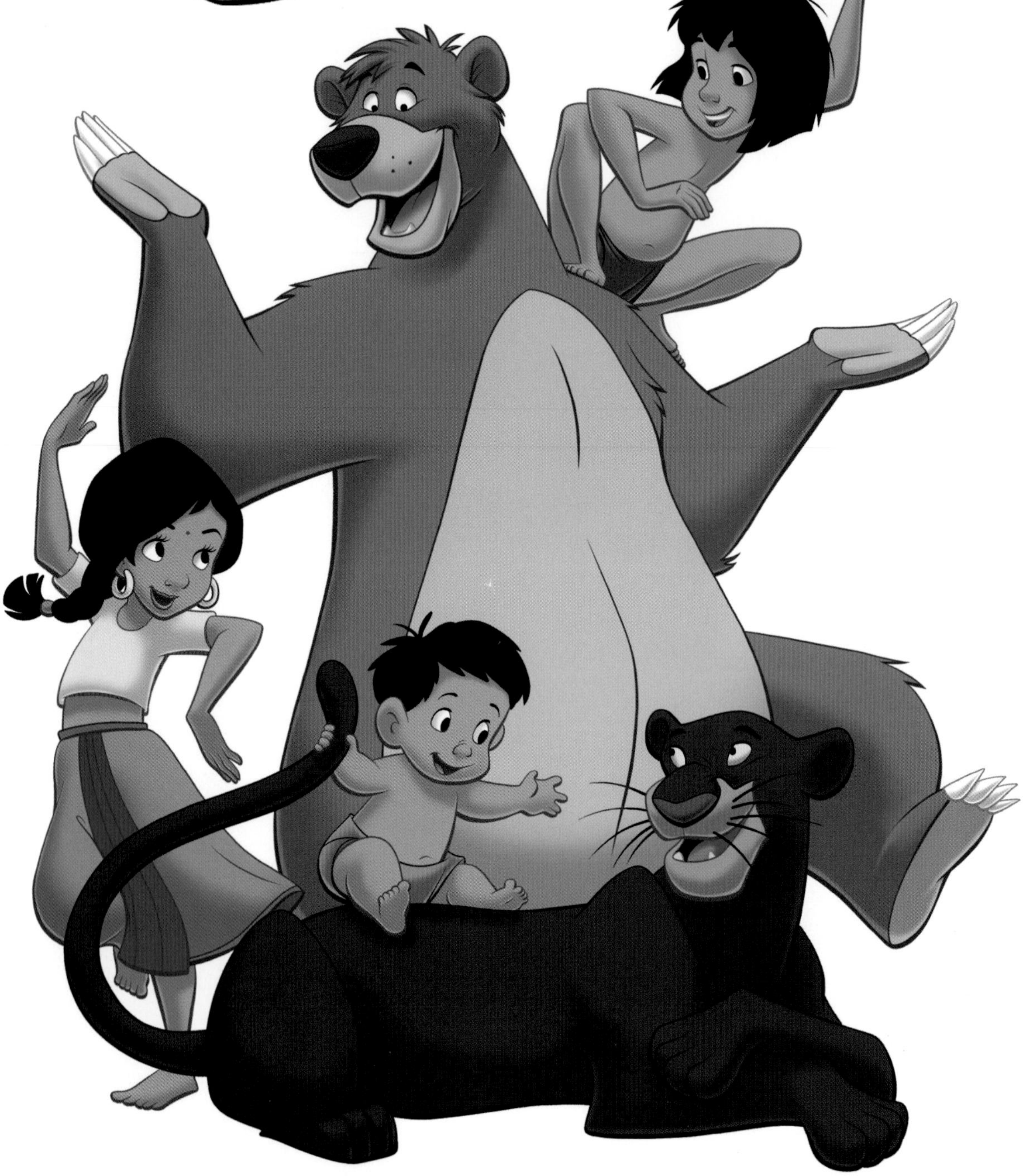

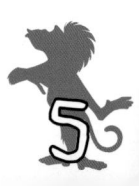

CONTENTS

DISNEY'S THE JUNGLE BOOK 2

Mowgli is living in the Man-village with his new friends, Shanti and Ranjan, but he still misses his big, cuddly friend, Baloo.

One evening, Mowgli put on a puppet show for his friends Shanti, her mother and little Ranjan. It was all about his animal friends from the jungle.

"ROOOAAAARRR!" yelled Ranjan at a puppet that looked like the ferocious tiger, Shere Khan. He leapt at the puppet screen and knocked it over. "I got him, Mowgli!" cried Ranjan.

"You sure did, Ranjan," said Mowgli. "But it's gonna be kinda hard to finish the story now."

"But we all know how it ends," teased Ranjan. "You see Shanti and you follow her into our village."

The adults decided it was time for bed. "'Night, Shanti," said Mowgli, as Shanti and her mother prepared to leave. "Watch out for Shere Khan on your way home."

"Everyone knows tigers don't come into the village," replied Shanti.

"Tigers go wherever they want," said Ranjan. "ROOOAAAARRR!"

Very early the next morning, Ranjan crept into Mowgli's room. They had big plans for the day!

The boys raced towards the river, arriving seconds before Shanti. "I'm on the lookout," Mowgli told her. "Yesterday, I saw tiger tracks here!"

"Tiger tracks?" asked Shanti.

"It's Shere Khan," whispered Mowgli. "And I hear he's looking for me, seeking revenge. So watch your back or the last thing you'll hear is..."

"ROOAARRRR!" cried Ranjan, as he leapt out of the bushes.

Shanti screamed and dropped her water jug. "You're horrible, stinky boys!" she cried, before dragging Ranjan off to pick mangoes.

"Why are you so scared of the jungle?" asked Ranjan. "Mowgli says..."

"You shouldn't listen to everything Mowgli says," said Shanti.

Just then, Mowgli appeared. "You wanna see a trick I learned in the jungle?" he asked, and he shot a banana out of its peel, right into Ranjan's mouth!

"Well, here's a trick learned right here at home," replied Shanti. She tossed a mango into the air. It caught on a branch and peeled itself on the way down.

"Wow, that's a neat trick!" cried Ranjan, excitedly.

"Like I said, Ranjan," Shanti went on, "don't listen to him."

Mowgli shrugged. "She's right, Ranjan," he said. "Don't listen to me. Listen to the jungle." He crouched down beside Ranjan. "Can you hear it?"

"Yeah!" cried Ranjan. "The jungle!"

"Yeah, man," said Mowgli. "And when you hear that rhythm, you get a crazy feeling inside."

The boys started dancing to the jungle rhythm. Soon the other village children were following them, dancing along. Even Shanti couldn't resist joining in.

Suddenly, Shanti realised where they were headed. "Stop! You're

crossing the river. You can't go in the jungle! It's too dangerous! Mowgli, STOP!" cried Shanti.

As Mowgli and the others stopped in surprise, Ranjan's father appeared. "Children, come inside this instant!" he shouted. "All of you!"

Then he showed Mowgli the scars on his arm from a ferocious tige

attack. "I am very disappointed in you," he said, sternly. "You put everyone in danger!"

Ranjan's father sent Mowgli to his room without any dinner. Shanti tried to apologize to Mowgli for getting him into trouble but Mowgli wouldn't listen.

Later, Mowgli stared out of the window of his room and watched the jungle treetops swaying in the distance. "Oh, Baloo," murmured Mowgli. How he missed his best friend! Would he ever see him again?

That same day, out in the jungle, Baloo was singing as he built a fake boy out of plant stems and a coconut. Bagheera the panther watched anxiously as the fake boy fell apart.

"This ain't gonna work; you just ain't Mowgli," sighed Baloo, sadly.

Bagheera closed his eyes and shook his head. "Poor fellow," he murmured. But when Bagheera opened his eyes, Baloo was gone! "Oh, no, not again!"

As Bagheera hurried off to find Baloo, a dark shadow fell across the jungle clearing.

It was Shere Khan, the tiger! This was where he had suffered his greatest defeat. Now he planned to have his revenge against the Man-cub, Mowgli.

Baloo didn't know that Shere Khan was nearby. All the big bear could think about was Mowgli so he headed for the river.

Bagheera cut him off. "It's not safe for Mowgli in the jungle," Bagheera reminded Baloo. "You know Shere Khan is looking for him."

Baloo pushed past him. "Outta the way, Baggy," he said.

But Bagheera didn't give up. He called Colonel Hathi, the elephant, and his troops. When they arrived, they chased Baloo along the river's edge, trying to keep him from crossing into the Man-village.

Finally, Baloo managed to slip away from the elephants. The only one who saw him was Colonel Hathi's son, Baby Elephant. He missed Mowgli, too. "This way, quick!" whispered the young elephant, helping Baloo to escape.

"Hey, thanks, kid," said Baloo, disappearing into the bushes.

Baloo headed towards the Man-village. All he wanted to do was find Mowgli and live together happily in the jungle, like they used to.

Baloo still had no idea that Shere Khan was nearby, let alone right here in the Man-village!

"Baloo!" shouted Mowgli, when he spotted his old friend.

Just then, Shere Khan came slinking around the corner. But at the same time, Shanti saw Baloo carrying Mowgli away!

"Help!" screamed Shanti. "There's a wild animal in the village!"

The villagers came running out of their homes. They saw Shere Khan and chased after him.

"Where are you going?" cried Shanti in confusion. "Come back! You're going the wrong way!"

Nobody was listening, so she grabbed a torch and ran after Mowgli and Baloo.

"Shanti, wait for me!" called Ranjan. But Shanti didn't hear him calling her.

Taking a deep breath, Shanti crossed the river into the jungle for the very first time. But there was no time to worry. Mowgli needed saving!

Continued on page 20...

13

Baloo's moves

Baloo is teaching Mowgli some fancy dance moves! Can you work out which move Baloo has made the most times?

a   b   c   d   e

Answer: c

Fun and games

Shanti, Ranjan and Mowgli always have plenty of fun together.
Can you find the answers to each of these puzzles?

1 Can you match each flower to its pair?

a b c d

e f g h

2 Which is the correct spelling of Mowgli's name?

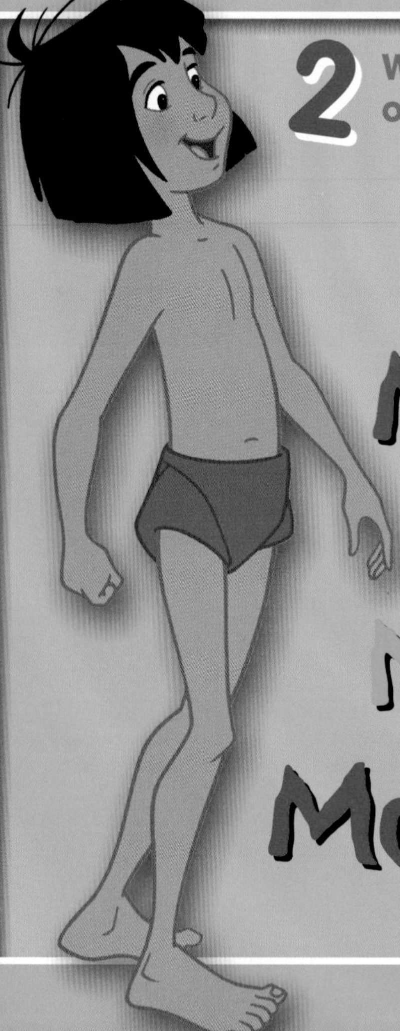

Mowglii

Mowgley

Mowgli

Mowgly

Mowwgli

Answers: 1) a-f, b-h, c-e, d-g. 2) Mowgli.

15

Snakes and ladders

It's dangerous in the jungle with Kaa, the snake, around. Play this game with your friends to find out who will be the first to dance through the jungle safely, to reach Baloo!

41	42	43	44	45
40	39	38	37	36
21	22	23	24	25
20	19	18	17	16
1 START	2	3	4	5

How to play

Place a counter each on START. Take it in turns to roll a dice and move your counter forward the number shown on the dice. If you land on the bottom of a ladder, climb to the top. If you land on Kaa's head, slide down to the bottom. The first player to reach Baloo is the winner!

6	47	48	49	50 FINISH
5	34	33	32	31
6	27	28	29	30
5	14	13	12	11
7	8	9	10	

17

Tiger alert!

How many times can you spot Shere Khan's shadow hiding on this page?

18

Jungle colouring

Can you add some jungle colours to this picture of dancing Baloo?

As Baloo and Mowgli wandered into the jungle, laughing and singing, Kaa spotted them. "Do my sssnake eyesss dec-ss-eive me?" he cried. "It's the sssucculent Man-cub!"

Unaware of Kaa, Baloo licked some tasty ants from the bottom of a rock. Then he tossed the rock to Mowgli.

"Thanks, Baloo," laughed Mowgli. He licked off a few ants, then threw the rock away, hitting Kaa right on his head!

Nearby, Shanti was nervously searching for Mowgli. The jungle was a scary place, full of dangers.

One of those dangers was the slithery Kaa.

Seeing Shanti coming, Kaa smacked his lips loudly "Who – who is it?" called Shanti, fearfully. "Who's there?"

"Are you lossst, little one?" asked Kaa. His eyes spun, hypnotizing her Just as Kaa was about to attack, a little hand reached out.

It was Ranjan!

He yanked Shanti away, knocking her out of Kaa's trance. "Bad snake!" shouted Ranjan, beating Kaa with a stick.

Moments later, Shere Khan found Kaa, lying where Ranjan and Shanti had left him.

"Where's the Man-cub!" growled Shere Khan. "I know you know."

Kaa didn't know where Mowgli was, but he didn't want Shere Khan to hurt him even more. "He'sss at the ssswamp!" said Kaa, quickly.

"He'd better be," said Shere Khan, with a low growl.

But Shere Khan wasn't the only one looking for Mowgli. The villagers were in the jungle, too, searching for all three missing children.

Colonel Hathi and his elephant troops heard the humans and panicked. They stampeded through the jungle, taking Bagheera with them!

"Shanti! Ranjan!" shouted the humans.

"Mowgli!" cried the village leader.

Suddenly, Bagheera realized what was happening. "Baloo!" he muttered, shaking his head.

Mowgli with a smile.

Just then, Baloo saw Bagheera coming towards them. He leapt in front of Mowgli, hiding him from sight.

"Man is in the jungle. They're searching for Mowgli. I thought that perhaps you would have seen the boy," said Bagheera.

"Me? No, you know his future is in that village," said Baloo, trying to cover up.

"I wonder if Shanti's with them?" said Mowgli, after Bagheera left

"Shanti?" exclaimed Baloo. "You don't want her to find you, do ya?"

Mowgli realised his old friend was right. He didn't need Shanti, or any of the villagers.

"What if that girl tracks us down?" Baloo asked.

"Then you're going to have to scare her," Mowgli decided.

Mowgli didn't realise all the trouble he was causing. He and Baloo were busy picking mangoes for breakfast. "Hey, check this out," said Mowgli. He tossed a mango into the air, just as Shanti had done, so it peeled itself on the way down.

"Not bad!" said Baloo. "Where'd you learn to do that?"

"Shanti showed me," replied

Meanwhile, Shanti and Ranjan were lost in the jungle. Shanti was very worried as she knew just how dangerous the jungle could be.

Shanti sat down and tried to work out where they were. She made a map out of sticks and stones. "Okay, here's the village," she muttered. "We crossed the river and . . . um . . ."

Ranjan was looking around the clearing. Suddenly, he spotted a long coil of mango peel.

"Ranjan?" asked Shanti. "What have you found?"

Shanti gasped when she saw the mango peel. "It's Mowgli!" she cried. "He must have been here!"

Meanwhile, Shere Khan had just reached the swamp. He sniffed the air and looked around but there was no sign of the Man-cub.

"That snake lied to me!" growled Shere Khan, menacingly.

Some vultures were watching Shere Kahn from up in a tree. "We heard that kid is here in the jungle, right under your whiskers," one of them told Shere Khan. "They say he's headed down river with a bear."

"Down river, you say?" The tiger smiled and dashed off. He was determined to find the Man-cub and teach him a lesson.

Continued on page 30...

23

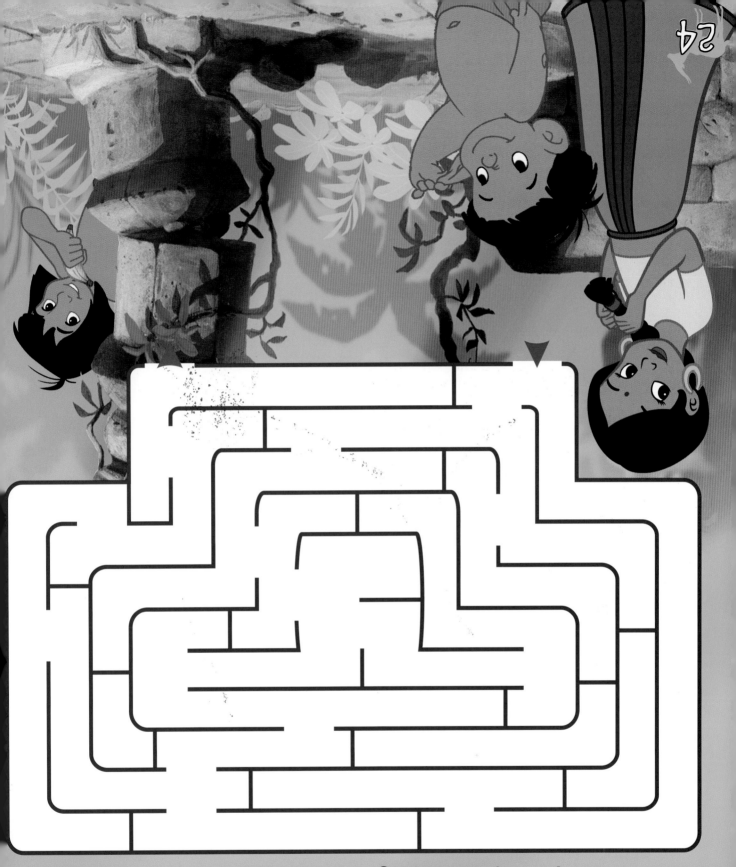

Through the maze

Ranjan and Shanti are in the jungle looking for Mowgli.
Can you help them through the maze to find him?

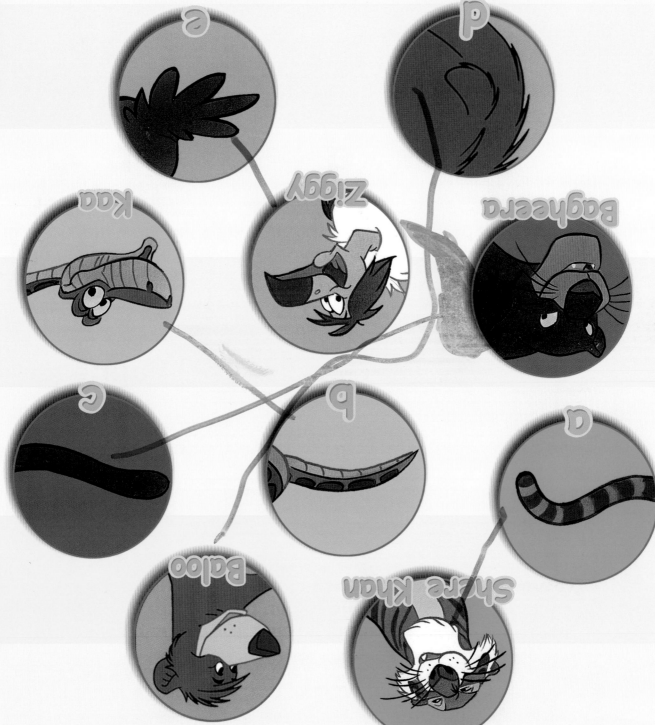

Head to tail!

Mowgli doesn't have a tail like his other friends in the jungle!
Can you see whom each tail belongs to? Draw lines to link them.

Jungle survival!

Mowgli knows that the jungle is a dangerous place with Shere Khan on the prowl, but it doesn't stop him from having fun!

Use your senses

To be fully alert Mowgli uses all his five senses – sight, smell, taste, touch and hearing.
What have you done today to use each of your five senses?

sight

smell

taste

touch

hearing

Who's hiding where?

In the jungle it's always useful to find yourself a good hiding place!
Can you work out who is hiding behind each of these pillars?

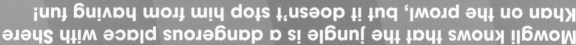

a   b   c

Answer: a-Shanti, b-Kaa, c-Baloo.

Survival snack

Bananas are a great survival snack because they not only taste good, but give you lots of energy, too! Here's how you can make some extra special survival bananas that can even help to keep you cool!

You will need: a banana, a lolly stick, honey, chocolate flakes, desiccated coconut.

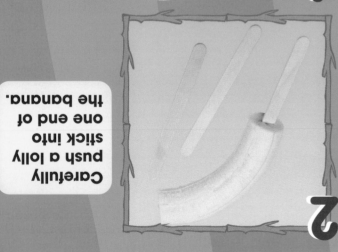

1 Peel a banana and cut a small piece off each end.

2 Carefully push a lolly stick into one end of the banana.

3 Brush an even amount of honey over the banana.

4 Sprinkle the chocolate flakes and coconut over the banana so that they stick to the honey.

5 Put the banana on a baking tray covered with cling film and ask an adult to put it in the freezer.

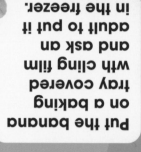

Bananas taste so good!

Answer:
1) Baloo's missing fruit. 2) Colour of Baloo's fruit. 3) Mowgli's missing fruit. 4) Colour of Mowgli's fruit.
5) Missing purple leaves. 6) Extra yellow flower. 7) Colour of Mowgli's shorts.
8) Colour of flower between Baloo and Mowgli. 9) Shere Khan's nose. 10) Mowgli's hand position.

Can you spot the ten differences in the bottom picture?

Spot the differences

Kaa's colours

Kaa is having a colourful time up in the tree! Can you follow the colour sequence in the circles to finish colouring him in?

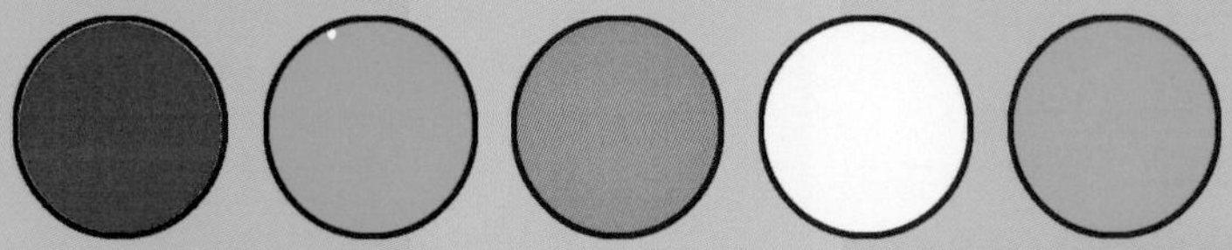

Answer: Orange, yellow, blue, red, blue, yellow, blue.

...Continued from page 23

The vultures were right. Baloo had taken Mowgli down river to an abandoned temple filled with chattering monkeys.

As a baboon band started to play, Baloo danced off into the crowd. Mowgli followed, his toes tapping to the beat.

"They don't swing out like that in your Man-village, now do they, kid?" a monkey asked Mowgli.

"Well, no," replied Mowgli. As the monkeys asked more questions, Mowgli started to feel bad. They made it sound like the Man-village was a terrible place to live!

Finally, Mowgli slipped away from Baloo and the monkeys. He wanted to think about where he really belonged. He climbed on to a tree branch with a view of the Man-village and started to think.

As Shanti and Ranjan continued searching for Mowgli, they suddenly heard sad singing from up ahead.

"Mowgli!" cried Ranjan, happily.

He and Shanti found Mowgli sitting up in the tree. Mowgli was very surprised and excited to see them.

Just then, Baloo appeared and saw Shanti. "It's her!" he gasped. Baloo remembered what Mowgli wanted him to do. "ROOOAAAARRR!" he cried as he charged towards them.

"Baloo, don't!" cried Mowgli. But it was too late.

Shanti was angry. How dare this wild animal kidnap Mowgli and try to scare her? She stepped forward and punched Baloo right in the nose.

All of a sudden, Shanti realized what was going on. "You planned this?" she demanded, glaring at Mowgli. Shanti grabbed Ranjan and stormed off.

Mowgli caught up with Shanti a moment later. Her eyes were wide and frightened. Mowgli turned and immediately saw why. Shere Khan was slinking towards them!

"You seem surprised to see me, Man-cub," laughed Shere Kahn.

Mowgli jumped in front of Shanti and Ranjan, trying to protect them. "Run," whispered Mowgli to the others.

Mowgli and his friends raced through the jungle to some big bushes. "Stay here," Mowgli told them.

"Mowgli, no!" cried Shanti. But Mowgli had already run off, with Shere Khan in hot pursuit.

"Ranjan, wait here," said Shanti. "I've got to help Mowgli!"

Ranjan did as Shanti said, for about two seconds. Then he followed the others.

As he pushed through some bushes, his shorts became caught on a branch. He flipped over and landed on the ground. Looking up, Ranjan gasped. A huge bear was standing over him!

"Whoa, calm down, kid," said Baloo, picking up the boy. "Now, where's Mowgli?"

"Shere Khan!" said Ranjan.

"Shere Khan?" exclaimed Baloo. "Hold on!" He put Ranjan on his shoulders, and rushed to the rescue.

Mowgli was still doing his best to stay ahead of Shere Khan. He reached the ruins of an ancient city and hurried up some stone steps into a giant theatre. He looked around for a place to hide.

A second later, Shere Khan appeared. "No matter how fast you run, no matter where you hide, I will catch you," said Shere Khan, with a growl. "Come out, come out, wherever you are!"

As Baloo and Ranjan searched for Mowgli, they ran into Bagheera. The panther was startled to see another Man-cub.

"Take the kid, Baggy," panted Baloo, handing Ranjan over to Bagheera just outside the ruined city. "I'll help Mowgli."

"Baloo," called Bagheera. "Be careful!"

Baloo nodded. Then he entered the ruins.

"Mowgli?" whispered Baloo, when he heard a noise. "Is that you?"

Baloo rounded a corner and ran straight into Shanti!

"You!" they both cried.

They started to argue but then they realised they were both there for the same reason; to help their friend.

"All right," said Baloo, to Shanti. "You go that way, I'll cover you."

Baloo hid behind a giant gong, then he saw Mowgli dive behind another gong. The three friends tricked Shere Khan by ringing three different gongs.

Soon, the confused tiger was running in circles, chasing the sounds of the ringing gongs.

Suddenly, Shanti's gong collapsed. "No more games, Man-cub," growled Shere Khan.

Mowgli and Shanti raced up a set of steps while Baloo leapt out and tried to distract Shere Khan.

But Shere Khan would not be distracted. He chased Mowgli and Shanti on to a ledge, overlooking a pit of boiling lava.

Shere Khan roared as he closed in. The Man-cub was about to be his!

"Mowgli, look out!" cried Baloo.

As Shere Khan leapt at them, Mowgli and Shanti jumped across the lava pit on to a giant stone tiger's head.

Shere Khan followed, but his weight was too much for the crumbling stone, and the head collapsed.

Luckily, Baloo's big paws grabbed Mowgli and Shanti, just in

time, and he pulled them to safety.

Mowgli and Shanti looked down at the pit. Shere Khan had landed on a stone pedestal sticking out of the lava. The tiger was trapped!

Shere Khan roared with fury. How would he ever be able to escape from this terrible place?

A few minutes later, Mowgli, Baloo and Bagheera and Shanti watched as Shanti and Ranjan raced off to meet the villagers.

Suddenly, Mowgli realised where he really belonged.

"Oh, Baloo," he murmured sadly. Baloo guessed what was coming. "It's okay, kid," he said. "That

girl isn't so bad after all, now, is she?" He paused. "Go on, Mowgli."

Mowgli grabbed Baloo, burying his face in the bear's fur. They hugged for a long moment. "I'm gonna miss you, Papa Bear," said Mowgli.

"Me too, Li'l Britches," replied Baloo, with a sniffle. "Me too."

Back at the Man-village, life went on as usual. Well, almost as usual.

"Come on, Mowgli," called Shanti. "We'll be late!"

Mowgli grabbed a large water jug. "I'm right behind you."

They told the adults they were going to fetch water. Then they raced to the river and skipped across the stepping-stones to the jungle side. Ranjan popped out of Mowgli's jug.

"Let's remember to actually bring back some water," said Mowgli to the others.

As they drummed on the empty jugs, Baloo emerged from the jungle.

"Hiya, Papa Bear!" called Mowgli, happily.

Soon, Bagheera appeared, too. Ranjan hopped on the panther's back as Baloo, Mowgli and Shanti danced to the jungle rhythms.

Mowgli finally knew where he belonged. He belonged with all of his friends – wherever they might be.

The end!

 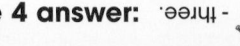

Win a magical family holiday to DISNEYLAND RESORT PARIS

*Imagine a land where the wonderful world of Disney comes alive.
Imagine two fantastic Theme Parks: **Disneyland® Park**, where you'll believe
in make-believe and where your favourite Disney characters are real!
Walt Disney Studios® Park, where the magic of Disney meets the fascinating
world of movies, television and animation.
Come and live the magic at **Disneyland® Resort Paris!***

**For a Disneyland® Resort Paris
free brochure, or to book, call
08705 030303 or visit
www.disneylandparis.co.uk**

**To enter, just answer this
simple question:
What is the name of
Baloo's Man-cub friend?**

The Prize Includes:
Return travel for 2 adults and
2 children (aged 3-11) plus 3
nights accommodation at a
Disneyland® Resort Paris
hotel including breakfast, 4
days unlimited admission into
the Disneyland® Park and
Walt Disney Studios® Park,
1 family Character Breakfast.

**Write your name, address and age on
a postcard or the back of a sealed
envelope and post to this address:
Egmont Books Limited (Disneyland
Resort Competition), 239 Kensington
High Street, London, W8 6SA.**

The closing date for entries is 23rd January 2004